THINK LIKE AN ENGINEER

ROBIN KOONTZ

Rourke
Educational Media

rourkeeducationalmedia.com

Before & After Reading Activities

Teaching Focus:

Have students locate the ending punctuation for sentences in the book. Count how many times a period, question mark, or exclamation point is used. Which one is used the most? What is the purpose for each ending punctuation mark? Practice reading these sentences with appropriate expression.

Before Reading:

Building Academic Vocabulary and Background Knowledge

Before reading a book, it is important to set the stage for your child or student by using pre-reading strategies. This will help them develop their vocabulary, increase their reading comprehension, and make connections across the curriculum.

1. *Read the title and look at the cover. Let's make predictions about what this book will be about.*
2. *Take a picture walk by talking about the pictures/ photographs in the book. Implant the vocabulary as you take the picture walk. Be sure to talk about the text features such as headings, the Table of Contents, glossary, bolded words, captions, charts/diagrams, or index.*
3. *Have students read the first page of text with you then have students read the remaining text.*
4. *Strategy Talk – use to assist students while reading.*
   - *Get your mouth ready*
   - *Look at the picture*
   - *Think…does it make sense*
   - *Think…does it look right*
   - *Think…does it sound right*
   - *Chunk it – by looking for a part you know*
5. *Read it again.*

Content Area Vocabulary
Read the list. What do these words mean?

ancient
biomimicry
categories
chemical
dementia
inaccessible
instincts
mechanical
obstacles
resources

After Reading:

Comprehension and Extension Activity

After reading the book, work on the following questions with your child or students to check their level of reading comprehension and content mastery.

1. *What are some of the obstacles that an engineer faces when working on a design? (Summarize)*
2. *The automatic bread slicer was invented to make slicing bread easier. What other things have been engineered to make life easier in the kitchen? (Asking Questions)*
3. *How has engineering changed your life in the past year? (Text to self connection)*
4. *Name a problem we have today that you think engineers should work on. What are your ideas to solve it? (Asking Questions)*

Extension Activity

Engineers get many of their ideas from nature. Read about one of the following animals and their abilities. Think of how that animal might inspire an engineer to design something useful: gecko, spider, bat, snake, shark, snail, centipede.

Table of Contents

What Are You Thinking?

   Have you ever taken something apart to see how it works? Do you like to figure out better ways to do things? Do you like science and math? If you answered yes to any of these questions, you might think like an engineer!

Engineers are the reason we have everything from thumbtacks to rocket ships. Our society depends on engineers to design everything we need to survive.

Communication, transportation, housing, medical care, and food are all improved by engineers. They find ways to help make the world a better and safer place to live.

An engineer thinks about problems and ideas for solving them. The process begins with three questions: What is the problem? Who has the problem? Why is the problem important to solve?

Engineers work to turn an idea into a reality. It doesn't matter how challenging the idea seems. If the problem is important to solve, it's worth a try. An engineer never thinks, "It can't be done." Instead, an engineer thinks, "How can I accomplish this?"

The Panama Canal

The Panama Canal was engineered in the late 1800s to connect the Atlantic Ocean to the Pacific Ocean. This 48 mile (77 kilometer) engineering wonder created an important route in maritime trade.

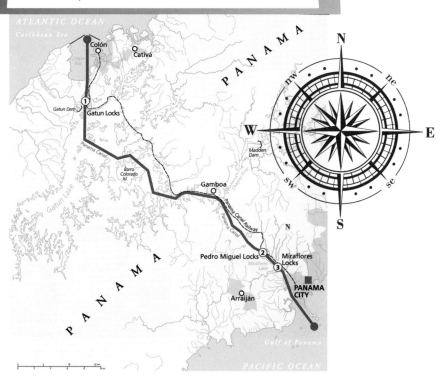

Most of the time, engineers think about improving something that already exists. For example, early engineers used a bone as a knife. Later, they sharpened a stone, which worked better than a bone. But after steel was engineered, knives became even better. Pretty soon, knives evolved into blades for all kinds of tasks.

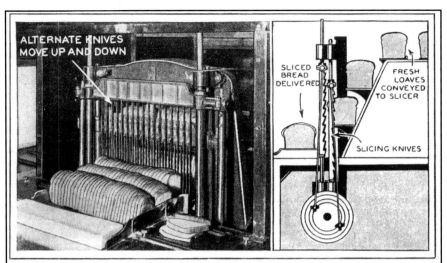

ALTERNATE KNIVES MOVE UP AND DOWN

SLICED BREAD DELIVERED

FRESH LOAVES CONVEYED TO SLICER

SLICING KNIVES

Sketch above shows how fresh bread loaves are conveyed through the slicing knives. Photo is a close-up of the slicer showing the double bank of keen, jagged knives, delivering the sliced loaves.

Inventive Engineering

Sliced bread wasn't available to purchase until an engineer named Otto Rohwedder designed and built an automatic bread slicer. It was one of the first engineered inventions that made life easier in the kitchen.

Engineers use their **instincts** along with knowledge of natural laws, scientific evidence, mathematics, and technology. But they are often faced with **obstacles**.

One obstacle can be costs. Experimenting with new ideas can be expensive. Add to that another obstacle: **resources**. Are the resources available to make the idea work? If not, what can the engineer use instead? What will it cost?

Human nature can be one of the biggest obstacles for engineers. People usually don't like change. If the same old thing works just fine, why fix it? Especially if it costs more money or is difficult to learn! Engineers deal with these and a lot of other obstacles.

A History of Great Thinkers

Three periods in the earliest human history are named for important engineering successes. The Stone Age was when tools and other useful items were chipped and carved from stone.

Next came the Bronze Age, when **ancient** engineers figured out how to melt copper and tin to make weapons and tools. The Iron Age came next when engineers began creating tools and machinery from iron.

Bronze Age household tools

Early engineers used limited resources to design and build houses, buildings, streets, and bridges along with heating, sewage, and water systems.

Engineering Marvel
The Great Pyramid of Giza was constructed during the Bronze Age. Clever engineers figured out how to design and build the massive structure with amazing accuracy. The 4,500-year-old pyramid still stands today.

The Great Pyramid of Giza is the largest and oldest of the three pyramids in the Giza pyramid complex bordering El Giza, Egypt.

Originally, there were four branches of engineering. **Mechanical** engineers design and often build machines. **Chemical** engineers deal with chemical processes. Civil engineers work on projects and systems that serve the public. Electrical engineers develop electrical equipment. Each of these branches has several **categories** for particular engineering jobs. There are now other kinds of engineers, such as software, computer, biomedical, and aerospace. And there are many more categories in each branch.

Learning from Disaster
The collapse of the Tacoma Narrows Bridge is often considered the most dramatic failure in bridge engineering history. Most engineers know about the incident because it is taught in their engineering classes.

Teamwork

Usually no single engineer designs a system. The project is divided up into several engineering branches. In a highway project, the goal is to map out a way that traffic can flow smoothly, no matter how many cars are on the road. Such a project starts with research engineers.

These engineers use experimentation, math, and science to research possible solutions. They provide their findings to design engineers, who select the methods and materials needed to make it all work. Next, construction engineers think of the ways production of the road system can be accomplished. Once the design is complete, construction work can begin. However, engineers stay involved in the project until it is completed.

FUN FACT!
One of the first computers was the Electronic Numerical Integrator Analyzer and Computer (ENIAC), built in the 1940s. It took a team of engineers to keep the 30-ton (27 metric ton) machine running.

Learning From Nature

Engineers learn by observing and thinking about nature. Birds gave them ideas for flight, beavers showed them ways to construct dams, and bats taught them about sonar.

FUN FACT!
Martha J. Coston designed a signal flare in 1859 that is still used today.

Biomimicry refers to the many engineering solutions inspired by the millions of time-tested feats of nature. Biomimicry has provided engineers with a vast array of tricks adaptable for designs of all kinds.

Nature's Inspiration   Biomimicry

Termite Mound   Self-cooling Building

The Eastgate Centre in Harare, Zimbabwe, is ventilated, cooled and heated entirely by natural means. The building was engineered based on a termite mound design.

Burrs   Velcro

An electrical engineer named George de Mestral noticed that burrs from burdock plants stuck to his dog. He later invented Velcro, one of the most widely used fastening systems in human history.

Kingfisher   Quieter High-Speed Train

The Shinkansen 500 high-speed train produced loud booms when roaring through narrow tunnels. Engineers redesigned the front-end to match a kingfisher's beak, which the fast-diving bird uses to silently splash into the water.

Some of the most amazing engineering designs are robots. Robots can replace people and animals in dangerous military and disaster situations. They can also go places that would otherwise be **inaccessible**.

Underwater Exploration

Unmanned underwater vehicles were first developed in 1957. Since then, engineers have developed remotely operated underwater vehicles (ROVs) and autonomous underwater vehicles (AUVs). They can provide information about places that could not otherwise be explored.

Many robots were inspired by nature. "Cheetah-bot" is a super-fast bot that imitates the world's fastest land mammal. RHex is fashioned after a cockroach. It can climb stairs and even flip over if it lands on its back.

The Legged Squad Support System (LS3) was built for rough terrain and designed to go anywhere a soldier goes, carrying up to 400 pounds (181 kilograms) of gear.

Spot the robot dog is smaller, faster, and quieter than the LS3. It is capable of carrying small loads and performing simple tasks.

The Sand Flea Robot is a four-wheeled robot that can roll forward, stop, turn, and go backward. It can also leap up about 30 feet (9 meters)! This skill lets the little wheel bug jump over walls and send video back to the humans while it's airborne.

Studying and learning from nature has contributed to new ideas in just about every branch of engineering.

Designing Drones
Drones are unmanned robotic aircraft. Drone engineers have been inspired by bats, swans, falcons, butterflies, dragonflies, bumblebees, hummingbirds, and even maple seeds.

Becoming an Engineer

What do you need to learn on your path to becoming an engineer? You can study and read about science, math, and technology. You can visit technology museums.

You can get involved with local Science Fairs and other invention challenges. But all you really need to do is think like an engineer: what problems would you like to solve? How would you solve them?

The annual Junior Solar Sprint in San Diego, California, challenges students to use science, creative thinking, experimentation, and teamwork to design and build solar-powered model cars.

Children from around the world have designed life-changing engineering projects. A Dutch teenager designed a platform that captures plastic garbage in the ocean. Another teen developed a test to detect pancreatic cancer. And a 15-year-old invented a wireless sensor that helps keep track of patients with **dementia**.

Boyan Slat (b. 1994) is the founder and CEO of The Ocean Cleanup, a company that develops technologies to rid oceans of plastic waste.

Engineering technology is expanding so fast there has probably never been a better time to enter the field. Just about everything people need requires the wise thinking of an engineer. The future depends on engineers to continue to make the world a better and safer place to live.

Modern Engineering
The most popular, successful, and influential results of engineering in modern times are probably computers and smartphones.

Activities

Here's your chance to think and work like an engineer!

Activity 1: Airplane Launcher

You will need:

• paper airplane (*www.foldnfly.com*)

• two 3-inch (7.62 centimeter) nails

• hammer

• rubber band

• wooden board that is wider than the airplane

What you do:

1. Hammer the two nails into the board, spaced wide enough for the plane to pass through.

2. Loop the rubber band over each nail so it stretches across.

3. Place the back of the airplane at the rubber band.

4. Pull back the rubber band and the plane, and let it fly!

Activity 2: Think, Design, Create

Imagine that you are an engineer faced with a problem.

1. What is the problem? What are the obstacles? You can use the airplane launcher as your problem, or something new.

2. What are some possible solutions?

3. Draw a plan and make a list of everything you will need to make it happen. How much will it cost? How much time will it take?

4. If materials are available, make it and test it. If not, figure out the costs and alternative materials to try. Create a marketing plan for your new product. Why would people buy it?

5. Write down the pros and cons of your design. If you tested your design, did it work? If not, did you change anything and try again?

Glossary

ancient (AYN-shunt): belonging to a time long ago

biomimicry (bye-oh-MIM-ik-kree): the act of mimicking nature

categories (KAT-uh-gor-eez): groups of things with something in common

chemical (KEM-uh-kuhl): a substance used in chemistry

dementia (di-MEN-shuh): a disorder of the brain that causes memory loss and other problems

inaccessible (in-ak-sess-uh-buhl): a place with no access

instincts (IN-stingkts): behavior that is natural rather than learned

mechanical (muh-KAN-uh-kuhl): to do with machines or tools

obstacles (OB-stuh-kuhls): things that get in the way or prevent you from doing something

resources (ri-SORSSES): things that are valuable or useful to a place or person

Index

Show What You Know

1. Why do we need engineers?

2. Name the four original branches of engineering. What does each one do?

3. When was the Great Pyramid of Giza built?

4. What are the three questions an engineer asks first?

5. What is an example of biomimicry?

Websites to Visit

www.engineergirl.org

www.sciencebuddies.org

www.sciencekids.co.nz/engineering.html

About the Author

Robin Koontz is a freelance author/illustrator/ designer of a wide variety of nonfiction and fiction books, educational blogs, and magazine articles for children and young adults. Her 2011 science title, *Leaps and Creeps - How Animals Move to Survive*, was an Animal Behavior Society Outstanding Children's Book Award Finalist. Raised in Maryland and Alabama, Robin now lives with her husband in the Coast Range of western Oregon where she especially enjoys observing and learning about the wildlife on her property as well as coming up with new ways to do things. You can learn more on her blog: robinkoontz.wordpress.com.

Meet The Author!
www.meetREMauthors.com

www.rourkeeducationalmedia.com

PHOTO CREDITS: Cover and title page ©suriya silsaksom; table of contents ©stockphoto mania; p.4 ©fstop123; p.5 and 6 ©3DSculptor; p.7 ©PeterHermesFurian; p.8 ©ferrantraite; p.9 ©Wiki, ©Johnn Scott; p.10 ©Terminator3D; p.11 ©Lisa-Blue; p.12 ©Mark Kositch; p.13 © Stanislav Khokholkov; p.14 © WitR; p.16 © Mckyartstudio; p.18 ©Faultier (bat), ©softlights3 (flame); p.19 ©Fat Jackey (termite mound), ©buffy123 (burrs), ©Leopardinatree (Kingfisher), ©Wiki (building), ©stocksnapper (velcro), ©JAKUB HALON (train); p.20 ©NOAA; p.21 ©DARPA; p.22 courtesy U.S. Department of Defense; p.23 ©LALS STOCK (drone), ©alslutsky (dragonfly); p.24 ©Blend Images; p.25 ©oconnelll; p.26 ©Erwin Zwart/The Ocean Cleanup; p.27 ©DGLimages (student), ©ahmetemre (electronics)

Edited by: Keli Sipperley
Cover and Interior design by: Rhea Magaro-Wallace

Library of Congress PCN Data

Think Like an Engineer / Robin Koontz
 (Science Alliance)
  ISBN 978-1-68342-346-1 (hard cover)
  ISBN 978-1-68342-442-0 (soft cover)
  ISBN 978-1-68342-512-0 (e-Book)
Library of Congress Control Number: 2017931190

Rourke Educational Media
Printed in the United States of America,
North Mankato, Minnesota